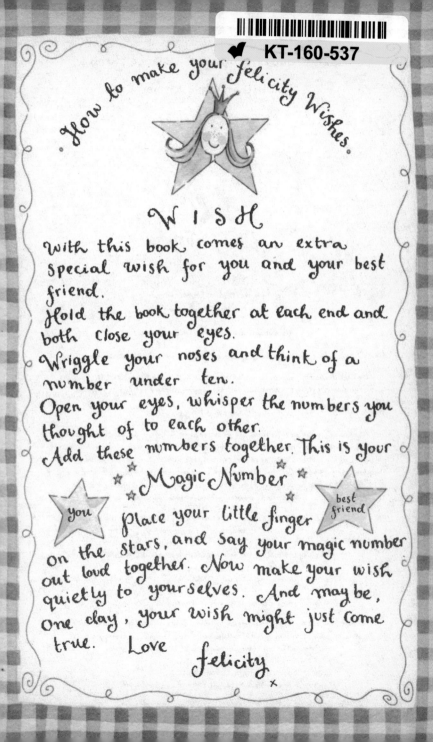

How to make your felicity Wishes.

W I S H

With this book comes an extra special wish for you and your best friend.

Hold the book together at each end and both close your eyes.

Wriggle your noses and think of a number under ten.

Open your eyes, whisper the numbers you thought of to each other.

Add these numbers together. This is your

✸ ✸ Magic Number ✸

✸ ✸

you   best friend

Place your little finger on the stars, and say your magic number out loud together. Now make your wish quietly to yourselves. And maybe, one day, your wish might just come true.   Love

felicity

x

For Madeline Grace Maia Calthrop
with twinkling wishes
E.V.T

Emma Thomson's
felicity Wishes®

FELICITY WISHES
Felicity Wishes © 2000 Emma Thomson
Licensed by White Lion Publishing

Text and Illustrations © 2005 Emma Thomson

First published in Great Britain in 2005 by Hodder Children's Books

A Catalogue record for this book is available from the British Library

ISBN 0 340 90243 4

Printed and bound in Great Britain by Bookmarque Ltd, Croydon, Surrey

The paper and board used in this paperback by Hodder Children's Books are natural recyclable
products made from wood grown in sustainable forests. The manufacturing processes
conform to the environmental regulations of the country of origin.

Hodder Children's Books
A division of Hodder Headline Ltd, 338 Euston Road, London NW1 3BH

Emma Thomson's felicity Wishes®

Whispering Wishes

and other stories

Hodder
Children's
Books

A division of Hodder Headline Limited

CONTENTS

Whispering Wishes

The Grand Wishmaker
will be appearing at the

Felicity Wishes, Holly, Polly and Daisy were crowded around the school notice board, along with a dozen other fairies, anxious to find out more about the visit from the Grand Wishmaker.

"I've heard she can do all sorts of amazing things," whispered Felicity in awe as she gazed up at a poster.

"Rumour has it that she can make herself disappear into thin air!" said Holly.

"Never!" exclaimed Daisy.

"She's more magical than any fairy I've ever known," said Polly, wide-eyed.

The
Grand Wishmaker

will be appearing at the

School of Nine Wishes

this Saturday only.

This is a unique opportunity to see real wish-making at its finest!

AMAZING feats, INCREDIBLE treats, and FANTASTIC wand magic to entertain and enthrall!

All week long a magical air filled the school. Everywhere you looked, fairies were enthusiastically reading the Grand Wishmaker's book: 'How to Make Impossible Wishes Come True', and practising swinging their wands in her unique loop-the-loop style.

"I saw her do this on television once," said Felicity, trying unsuccessfully to do a super-spin twist to make herself invisible. "Hmm, although I don't know quite how she did it!"

"It's pure magical talent," said Polly. She had studied the Grand Wishmaker's book down to the last star but even Polly was struggling to see any magical results.

"Some fairies just have 'it'," said Holly, who was more interested in working out how the Grand Wishmaker achieved her beautiful rainbow eyeshadow effect.

"And some just don't!" said Daisy, exasperated. She closed her book shut with a sigh and opened one on flowers instead. Daisy knew everything there was to know on flowers, so felt much happier reading a book on this subject.

"I've got an idea," said Felicity. "If we arrive really early on Saturday we can sit on the front row. That way we'll be able to see exactly how the Grand Wishmaker makes her magic wishes come true."

"Yes, and then we'll be able to do it ourselves!" added Polly. Polly was always good at everything and found it very frustrating that she hadn't been able to grasp the Grand Wishmaker's magic straight away.

"Don't you think every fairy in the School of Nine Wishes is thinking exactly the same thing?" asked Holly, gesturing around her at all the fairies

trying out the Grand
Wishmaker's wishes
without success.

"Well, we'll just
have to arrive
super-early then,"
said Felicity resolutely.

"Like the day before!"
joked Daisy.

"Now, that's not a bad
idea," said Felicity seriously.

Holly, Polly and Daisy groaned.
They didn't relish spending a night
sleeping in the school hall.

* * *

Friday soon came and excitement
at the school had reached fever pitch!
All anyone could talk about was the
Grand Wishmaker's performance the
next day. Even the teachers couldn't
contain their anticipation.

"There's been a change of plan for
our lesson today," announced Miss

Sparkle, the Chemistry teacher. "We're not going to have the test I set you. Instead, we are going to have a day of experimental wish-powder making!"

Everyone cheered.

"Some fairies believe that it is the wish-powder and not the wish-making that ensures the Grand Wishmaker's success with even the most impossible of wishes."

In Music, Miss Quaver had everyone creating a magical twinkly noise with their wand when it passed through the air to make wishes.

"Personally," she said earnestly to the class, "I think that sound is actually the secret of the Grand Wishmaker's success."

Even in Games class,

Miss Skipping made sure that the whole class was devoted to dainty footwork. She said it was for netball practice but everyone knew that the Grand Wishmaker recommended using subtle feet movements for successful wish-making.

* * *

By the time the last bell rang for the end of school on Friday the atmosphere was electric! Within seconds, every class was empty as fairies flew straight home to get an early night for the big day tomorrow. All except Felicity, Holly, Polly and Daisy, who secretly hid under the large staircase in the main hall.

"I think everyone's gone," whispered Felicity, listening intently.

"Are you sure?" whispered Polly cautiously.

"Yes, I even heard Fairy Godmother lock up," said Holly, poking her head out of the curtains and glancing round the hall.

The fairies slowly crept out from under the staircase and jiggled their cramped wings. It was rather tiny under the staircase and it had taken three attempts for all four fairies to squeeze into the space.

Even though they knew the school well, it felt like a very different place at night with no one around. Normally the hall was brimming with chattering fairies but tonight you could hear a wand drop! Dark, strange shadows filled the room and the fairies started to feel a little uneasy about spending the night there.

"I didn't realise the hall could look so big... and dark... and... scary," said Daisy nervously.

"I'm not one to get scared easily," said Holly. "But I would much rather be tucked up in my bed at home than here."

"I know, let's snuggle down into our sleeping bags and then we can tell funny stories to cheer each other up," said Felicity.

The fairies started to unpack their overnight bags: four sleeping bags, four pairs of pyjamas and slippers, four fluffy teddy bears and, most importantly, four bags of midnight snacks!

It wasn't long before the fairies were happily chatting and munching their sparkle bars.

Suddenly the air was filled with a deafening CRASH!

"What was that?!" said Daisy, sitting bolt upright.

"I don't know!" said Felicity, her voice shaking. "I'm sure everyone had gone home."

"Quick! Let's hide before we get caught," said Polly panicking, dragging the other fairies out of their sleeping bags.

Quickly they flew towards the nearest object – a large wicker basket – and jumped right into it! They quickly closed the lid tight and breathed a small sigh of relief.

"What was that?" asked Holly into the darkness.

"Shhh!" whispered Felicity, her wings still quivering. "I can hear voices!"

The fairy friends put their ears to the basket and listened carefully. They could hear voices and laughter and it was getting closer by the minute!

"What are we going to do?" asked Polly nervously.

"We'll stay put until they go," whispered Felicity. "No one make a noise."

The hall doors suddenly swung open to reveal four tall and very strong-looking fairies, carrying large boxes and bags. Felicity, Holly, Polly and Daisy peeped through the gaps in the basket.

"Are we setting the stage up like the show we did in Star Valley?" said one of the fairies.

One of the others got out a letter

from her pocket, unfolded it carefully, and showed it to the rest.

"The Grand Wishmaker says that she doesn't want any mistakes this time. The pulleys, mirrors, ropes and lights are to be positioned exactly as she's shown on this plan."

Hours and hours slowly passed by as Felicity and her friends watched intently as the stage was transformed for tomorrow's performance. Not daring to speak, they just looked at each other with raised eyebrows and shocked faces as the four tall fairies rigged each and every prop. Everything was measured to the millimetre before the four tall fairies decided where to position a certain mirror, or how to hang a particular rope.

When they had finally finished neither Felicity or her friends heard them go. They had all fallen sound asleep in the basket.

✳ ✳ ✳

"What's this basket doing here?" bellowed Fairy Godmother.

Felicity and her friends woke up with a start.

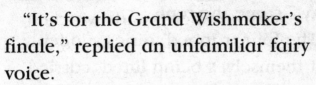

"It's for the Grand Wishmaker's finale," replied an unfamiliar fairy voice.

"Well it can't stay here in the middle of the room like this," grumbled Fairy Godmother. "We do have Health and Safety rules to follow."

"Of course," said the fairy. "We're just about to move it onto the stage."

"Well, be quick about it," said Fairy Godmother, looking at her watch. "You've only got an hour to go before the fairies are let in. Some have been here since eight o'clock this morning!"

Felicity, Holly, Polly and Daisy

looked desperately at each other, not knowing what to do. Suddenly, the fairies fell forward as the basket was lifted up at one side.

"Cilla, come and give me a hand. This feels heavier than before," came a voice from outside.

"It's not heavier, you're just feeling lazy!" came the reply.

The four trapped fairies suddenly felt themselves being lifted, carried across the room and then dumped on stage with a large thud!

"Actually, you're right. That did feel heavier," said the voice as it trailed off into the distance.

"At least we'll get a good view," said Polly, peeping through the basket to discover their prime location centre-stage.

"I'm not sure if I want one any more," said Holly, remembering what she'd seen the night before. "The

Grand Wishmaker doesn't make impossible wishes come true after all. She cheats with pulleys, ropes and mirrors."

"You don't know that for definite," said Felicity, who always believed the best in everyone.

"Yeah," said Daisy, also keen to believe the magic. "Maybe the props are for something else?"

But even before the hall had filled up Felicity and her friends saw what they didn't really want to believe – the Grand Wishmaker was being harnessed into a support that enabled her to fly without the use of her wings!

The fairies' wings drooped with disappointment as the heavy velvet stage curtains parted.

Felicity, Polly, Daisy and Holly watched from the basket as the Grand Wishmaker flew on to the stage to the rapturous applause of hundreds of

excited fairies. As the crowd's applause
grew, the Grand Wishmaker waved her
wand in her trademark loop-the-loop
way.

Suddenly she seemed to disappear.

Not into thin air, as she'd promised
the crowd, but behind a secret door
that only Felicity and her friends could
see from inside the basket.

When shouts from the audience

begged for her most famous wish, the Grand Wishmaker spun so fast she turned herself into stone. Only Felicity and her friends could see that it wasn't stone at all, but a dummy lowered expertly on pulleys into her place.

Even when the crowd went wild as the Grand Wishmaker made an identical double of herself, it was just the four fairy friends who could see it was a mirror trick.

"Thank you, thank you!" boomed the Grand Wishmaker to the crowd of cheering fairies, who were now standing on their chairs and clapping louder than ever!

"For my final wish I have saved the best until last. Can I have quiet please."

An excited hush descended on the hall.

"I am going to attempt to wish

myself into this basket in the blink of
an eye. It's a difficult wish that
demands complete concentration."

Felicity, Holly, Polly and Daisy
gulped.

The Grand Wishmaker closed her
eyes, raised her flowing sleeves high
above her head dramatically
and pointed her
wand towards
the basket.

A huge puff of smoke engulfed the
stage and the Grand Wishmaker was
gone!

As the curtain fell, a stunned silence

was shortly followed by loud cheers. Everyone went wild. Fairies everywhere were crying out for more. It was the most amazing wish they had ever seen.

What they hadn't seen was that the cloud of smoke had been triggered by a button underneath the Grand Wishmaker's foot. Then, as the stage filled with smoke, the Grand Wishmaker had dashed over to the basket, lifted the lid, and jumped in.

It was lucky that the squeals from Felicity and her friends when the Grand Wishmaker landed on them were drowned out by the cheering crowd.

"WHAT are you doing in here?!" blasted the Grand Wishmaker, flinging open the lid and jumping out.

"Watching your fake performance," said Polly, unable to contain her frustration.

"Yes," said Holly, enjoying the drama of the situation. "You can't make magic wishes at all."

At first the Grand Wishmaker looked awkward but then she straightened her wings proudly and looked them straight in the eye.

"You will learn that there are many different ways to make magic wishes come true. Those I made on stage were made for fun and you can see..." she said, opening the curtain just enough to show the happy, giggling fairies on the other side, "that a little bit of magic has come true today."

Felicity, Holly, Polly and Daisy had to agree. Even though the magic wishes might not have been done in the way they thought, everyone had enjoyed them just the same.

"People see what they want to believe, and that's the most powerful magic there is. More powerful than any wish powder, twinkly music or dainty footwork," said the Grand Wishmaker knowingly. "Let me show you exactly what I mean."

And with that she lifted her wand high into the air, made a super-spin twist, waved goodbye...

and then completely

disappeared

into thin

air!

Use trust to keep
secrets safe

and you'll always
be a good friend

Invisible Identity

Break-time for Holly usually meant a long visit to the powder room where she would brush her hair, touch up her make-up and cover herself in a cloud of petal perfume before joining her friends for a gossip and a giggle.

This break-time, however, Holly was being unusually studious. She dashed straight to the library after class and had her head in the books even before the other fairies had tucked into their break-time snacks!

"What are you doing in here?" whispered Felicity, shocked at seeing Holly in a library.

Holly lifted up a heavy book from the top of her pile – 'The Chemistry of Wishmaking'.

"Ever since we saw the Grand Wishmaker disappear into thin air right in front of our eyes," began Holly excitedly, "I've been determined to find out how she makes impossible wishes come true."

Felicity remembered back to the eye-opening show that had been held at the School of Nine Wishes some weeks ago. Most of the Grand Wishmaker's wishes had actually just been clever tricks, but even Felicity had to admit that her disappearing act was no illusion!

* * *

When Felicity, Holly, Polly and Daisy met up at Sparkles after school for a hot chocolate, Holly still had her nose in a book. She hadn't said a word to her friends since she arrived and that was very unusual behaviour for Holly.

"Are you any closer to turning yourself into a buttercup?" joked Daisy.

"No, no!" said Holly. Her gaze didn't leave the pages. "But I've found lots of remarkable theories on how the Grand Wishmaker makes herself disappear. It's really quite fascinating, you know."

"I wouldn't mind disappearing before our maths test tomorrow," said Felicity wishfully.

Holly looked up. "This is no joking matter, Felicity!" she said quickly. "Wishmaking is a serious art and some of the methods I'm reading about take years of careful preparation."

"Sorry, I was only being silly," said Felicity, looking down at her toes.

"So how do you make yourself disappear then?" asked Polly, trying to clear the air. "It must be quite difficult, or people would do it all the time."

Holly sat up proudly, pleased with the opportunity to show off what she'd learned in the last few days. "Well," she began, "to make yourself disappear it seems the conditions need to be just right." Holly pulled out a large leather-bound book from her bag and opened the marked page. "Firstly, you need a full moon."

Wishes and Wishmaking

Daisy jumped up. "It is a full moon today. Look!" she said, pointing out of the window at the early evening moon.

"You also need," said Holly, pausing to read the next section, "to be wearing clothes the colour of the season. So if it's autumn you have to wear something orange, and if it's spring something green."

"What a shame," said Polly, looking at Holly's yellow dress. "It's winter so I guess you should have been wearing red not yellow for the wish to work."

"That's not all though," said Holly. "Once you have all of those things in place, then you have to wave your wand above your head and repeat a magical wish off by heart without making a single mistake!"

"Oooh, why don't you try it!" said Felicity, bursting with excitement. "We can test you on your wish and, after all, you're not going to disappear altogether as you're not wearing the right colour, remember."

"Oh, OK," said Holly reluctantly. She had only read the wish a couple of times and was sure she wouldn't remember it now.

Felicity, Polly and Daisy huddled together on the sofa with the large leather-bound book between them, focusing on the words. Holly sat nervously in front of the fairies. She closed her eyes, took a deep breath and began:

"Beep-diddly-oden-boden-bodo schq-dute-en-daten,
Ish-bibbly-op and bob an boo bar an
Esterweeny Sallatweeny ooh ahhh le wallah weeny bip an bop an barish,
Amenta-Betamia, Tallah-doonah, shlap-a-not."

"You did it! Word perfect!" squealed Felicity, closing the book and jumping up to give Holly a big hug. "Holly, you did it... Holly? Where's she gone?"

Polly and Daisy looked behind the sofa, under the coffee table and all around Sparkles but Holly was nowhere to be seen!

"Maybe she's gone to get some fresh air," suggested Daisy, heading outside. "I'll go and find her and tell her the good news!"

"What are you talking about?" said Holly loudly. "I'm here!"

"Did you hear something?" said Daisy stopping in her tracks. "It sounded like Holly."

"I'm here!" said Holly even louder. "In front of you!"

Felicity, Polly and Daisy looked blankly at the space in front of them.

"Holly?" said Felicity, almost in a whisper. "Are you really here?"

"Of course I'm here," said Holly, impatiently. "Where else would I be?" she said.

Daisy's, Polly's and Felicity's mouths dropped as they watched Holly's hot chocolate float up into the air.

"What? Why the funny looks?" asked Holly, taking a sip of her hot chocolate. "Did I get it all wrong? I knew it! Making an impossible wish come true must take years of practice. And I'm not even wearing the right colour dress."

Felicity leaned towards Holly's voice. "Holly," she said quietly, "you got it completely right. YOU'RE INVISIBLE!"

"I can't be, I'm not wearing red," squealed Holly.

"But Holly you are invisible!" said Polly, her mouth wide-open with surprise.

"Really?" said Holly, her voice full of excitement.

"Really!" exclaimed Felicity, Polly and Daisy.

* * *

The enormity of what happened that afternoon didn't really sink in until the fairy friends met up for school assembly the following day.

"Has anyone seen Holly this morning?" asked Felicity concerned.

"I don't think anyone could possibly see Holly today!" said Daisy giggling.

Suddenly Felicity's crown pinged off her head!

"What was that?" asked Felicity spinning round.

"Holly? Is that you?" said Felicity under her breath.

Then Polly's crown pinged off!

"Don't!" said Polly. "Someone will notice!"

"No one will notice anything," said Holly, mischievously slipping off. "I'm invisible, remember!"

Fairy Godmother had barely begun to read her notices for the day when Felicity, Polly and Daisy had to stifle their giggles with their hands. With each sentence Fairy Godmother read, her long, flowing, shimmering skirt raised itself a little more. By the time she had started the 'lesson of the day' you could almost see her bloomers and the whole school, including most of the teachers, were in hysterics!

* * *

Holly's fun didn't stop there.

At break-time she eavesdropped on other fairies' gossip and at lunch-time she almost gave herself away giggling when she swapped her soggy jam sandwich with another fairy's delicious chocolate spread baguette.

But the best part of the day had to be Games lesson. Holly's team, Stars, always lost at netball but with the help of their invisible friend, it wasn't long before they won a victory they could boast about for years to come. The only sad part was not being able to join in the celebrations at the end of the game because no one knew she was there.

* * *

As the day went on, Holly discovered there were more disadvantages than advantages to being invisible.

"Lucky you being invisible for the maths test," whispered Felicity to Holly over her shoulder in class. "You can copy everyone's answers."

"I think that would be taking the invisibility thing a bit far!" said Holly, slightly shocked at Felicity's suggestion that she might cheat.

"Fairies, each of you should have a test paper in front of you," said Miss Pye, staring at Felicity who seemed to be talking to herself! "Just before we begin, does anyone know where Holly is today?"

The class turned to Felicity, Polly and Daisy but their stares were met with blank expressions from the fairy friends.

Holly put up her hand but quickly pulled it down again when she realised it was pointless. How would she ever explain her invisibility if no one could see her!

"Well, in that case, let's begin then," said Miss Pye.

Holly was also feeling rather

disappointed that no one had complimented her on her beautiful new dress. Holly, being a very fashion-conscious fairy, took great care of her appearance and was looking forward to showing off the sparkling creation. And, to top it all, Suzi Sparkle, the fairy diva, had worn the exact same dress in this week's edition of Fairy Girl.

Normally, every fairy in the School of Nine Wishes would be talking about Holly's outfit but being invisible meant that no one could see how glamorous she was looking, not even herself!

To cheer herself up, Holly flew to the Large Oak Tree in the playing fields for an afternoon snack of yummy chocolate sprinkles. She was only halfway through the pack when a group of fairies fluttered over and sat on her!

"I'm going to be covered in bruises at this rate," she grumbled to herself as she squeezed her way out from under a very tall fairy.

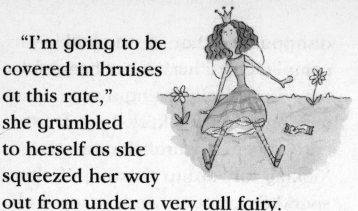

* * *

When Holly met Felicity, Polly and Daisy in Sparkles later on that afternoon, she was terribly down in the dumps. The novelty of being invisible had definitely worn off.

"I really don't like being invisible," said Holly glumly. "At first I thought it was fun but it soon became really boring. I've failed my maths test because I didn't turn up even though I did! No one has even noticed my beautiful new dress, and I'm covered in bruises from head to toe as fairies keep sitting on me!"

Felicity, Polly and Daisy tried to

control their giggles. They didn't like to see Holly down in the dumps but they kept imagining Holly being sat on!

"Maybe it's time to be visible again," suggested Felicity. "It's not the same without you!"

Holly said nothing but Felicity, Polly and Daisy could see her tears splashing on the coffee table in front of them.

"Holly?" said Felicity quietly. "Are you OK?"

"Yes," sniffed Holly. "It just that... I... don't know how to make myself visible again. I never reached that chapter in the book."

Felicity heaved Holly's heavy bag of wish books onto the table. "Well then, we shall stay here and read through these books until we do."

Holly's crown nearly pinged off with joy.

"Remember we've got ballet in ten minutes though," said Polly.

Felicity sighed. "Well, in that case," she said to Holly, "I'll meet you at your house when we're finished. I promise you'll be visible again soon."

* * *

Felicity's ballet class had gone so well, she had forgotten all about Holly's problem. It wasn't until she put her key in her front door that she suddenly remembered her promise. She quickly dumped her bags and was just about to fly off to Holly's house when she saw a familiar fairy approaching in the distance.

"You left these behind," said the waitress from Sparkles, handing Felicity Holly's large bag of wish books. "I thought someone was still there, but when I came to clear up your table for closing time you had all gone."

Felicity looked confused. "Thanks," she said taking the bag. "That's really kind of you. There was definitely no one left in the café when you shut up? You see I left earlier and these books belong to a friend."

"I thought I heard something just as I turned the key. But I double-checked through the window and there was no one there."

"Would you mind if I borrowed your keys to make sure?" asked Felicity, fearing the worst. "I'll bring them right back first thing tomorrow so you open in time."

"Well," said the waitress fairy, "it's not usual practice, but OK." And she handed over a bunch of keys to Felicity.

Within a wink, Felicity flew off with the heavy bag of books.

"Holly!" cried Felicity through the Sparkles café letterbox. "I know you're in there! I've got the key!" Frantically Felicity fumbled with the bunch of jangling keys until she found the right one. She put it in the lock, turned it and opened the door to see Holly standing in the doorway grinning!

"You did it! You're visible!" cried Felicity, hugging her friend tightly and dropping the heavy bag of books on the floor.

"How did you do it?" she squealed.

"It was all by accident really. When you went to ballet I found a quiet corner and stayed behind reading my books, trying to find out how to become visible again. I was just getting to a good bit when the waitress fairy came and took my books away!"

"So how did you know how to reverse the wish?" asked Felicity confused.

"Well, when she picked up my books, she accidentally knocked a leftover milkshake all over me," said Holly.

"So the spilt milkshake made you visible?" asked Felicity still confused.

"No, silly! When I went to the toilet to clean my skirt I discovered something magical. All you have to do to reverse an impossible wish, is to take away one of the things that made it happen in the first place."

Felicity looked blank.

"I was wearing a red petticoat!" said Holly triumphantly. "I had forgotten all about it, which is why the wish surprised us all by working in the first place. As soon as I took it off I became visible again!"

Felicity hugged her friend. "Fairy

Godmother has always said, 'Wishes come true when you least expect them'...all we have to do is believe!"

Some secrets are best kept

secret forever

Multiple Magic

Felicity Wishes and her friends, Holly, Polly and Daisy were sitting on large comfy sofas in Sparkles café, drinking frothy chocolate milkshakes and reading their favourite magazines.

"You'll never believe this!" exclaimed Felicity, waving Fairy Girl above her head.

"What?" asked Holly, dragging her eyes away from an article on 'How to Dress like a Fairy Star'.

"According to Fairy Girl, the fastest time a fairy has ever flown around

Fairy World was three days and fifteen hours!"

"Oooh, I bet her wings were tired afterwards!" said Daisy, wincing.

"There are lots of amazing facts in this article," continued Felicity. "You'll like this one, Polly – the biggest tooth ever collected by a tooth fairy was so big that fifteen fairies had to remove it from under the pillow!"

"What other interesting facts do you have there, Felicity?" asked Holly.

"Hmm, that's all it says here but apparently there are more facts in The Book of Fairy World Records," said Felicity.

"I've got that book at home somewhere," said Polly. "Why don't you all come round tomorrow for lunch and we can look up some more world records. I wonder who's got the record for making the most spectacular wish?"

"I bet it's the Grand Wishmaker," said Holly guessing. The fairies had seen her sensational wish-making skills last term.

"Well, we can find out tomorrow!" said Felicity closing her magazine and sipping the last drop of hot chocolate.

* * *

"Look, look!" shouted Felicity, fluttering through Polly's front door at a tremendous speed. She landed in the living room with a fairy-like thud, holding out a long, golden strand of hair. "I think I could enter The Book of Fairy World Records with this."

It certainly was the longest hair

any of the other fairies had ever seen before.

"Well," said Polly, flipping through the heavy book. "I'm afraid it doesn't look as though you're the only fairy to have super-long hair in Fairy World. I always thought that Fairy Godmother's hair was long, but there's a fairy here that can not only sit on her hair, but she can stand on it as well!"

The fairies moved in closer and looked at the old, grey picture of a tiny fairy with long straight hair that only stopped when it reached her toes!

"Never mind," said Felicity, a little disappointed, as she turned the page to discover yet more super-long hair records. There were courageous fairies with hair so strong they could use it as rope. There were fashion fairies with lengthy locks they'd piled high into weird and wonderful

STRONGEST HAIR

BIGGEST HAIR

LONGEST HAIR

MOST MAGICAL HAIR

hair-dos. There were even fairies whose hair was so heavy that they couldn't fly.

"That's a shame," said Holly. "It would have been super to be in The Book of Fairy Records for something extraordinary. We could have been famous!"

"Well, why don't we attempt to break a record for something else then?" offered Polly, who was quite taken with the idea herself.

The fairies pored over page after

page of amazing world records, trying to work out whether they could beat them.

"Look – there's a fairy world record for fitting the most fairies onto one cloud at once!" said Daisy, pointing to one entry.

"We could try and break the fairy world record for waving your wand above your head without stopping," said Holly.

"What about the fairy world record for loop-the-loop flying?" said Polly, feeling queasy just thinking about it.

After much discussion, they finally agreed that they couldn't beat the world record for anything sporty as the furthest they could run was to Sparkles after school.

Neither could they beat the world record for baking

cakes as they mostly bought theirs ready-made from The Sticky Bun. Or beat the world record for keeping quiet the longest – they couldn't imagine an hour let alone a day without a good gossip. The fairies sat back with a sigh.

"I've got it!" said Felicity, jumping forwards and lifting up the book triumphantly. "We should attempt to break the fairy world record for making the biggest wish!"

"That's a great idea!" chorused Holly, Polly and Daisy, springing to their feet with excitement.

"The current title holders live on Bird Island. Over two hundred fairies got together at the same time to wish for rain. Surely we can beat that?" said Felicity positively.

Holly, Polly and Daisy were not so sure.

* * *

That night, when they were all tucked up in bed, Felicity, Holly, Polly and Daisy dreamed of how to make a wish bigger than any they'd ever done before.

The next day, Felicity woke up with excited butterflies in her tummy.

"We can do this!" she said to herself in the bathroom mirror.

* * *

"It's no easy thing," said Fairy Godmother to the fairy friends who had sought her advice. "Big wishes involving lots of fairies are notoriously hard to organise. Think how hard it is to make up a dance routine when you all have to do the same steps together. Well, times that by two hundred and I'd say it's impossible. Maybe you should try something a little easier?"

And with that Fairy Godmother was off to teach her next lesson.

Felicity Wishes was not giving up

though. If the fairies on Bird Island could do it, then so could the School of Nine Wishes.

There were over three hundred fairies in the school, which should be plenty to secure them a place in The Book of Fairy World Records, as long as everything went to plan!

✳ ✳ ✳

All day at school, Felicity studied the rule book, desperately trying to work out how to beat the existing world record. By the end of the day, she had read it from cover to cover, made notes all over her homework book, and come up with a foolproof plan!

"OK, this is it!" she said excitedly to Holly, Polly and Daisy at school the next day. "Firstly, I've told the Fairy World Record judges that the School of Nine Wishes will be attempting to break a record this Saturday at twelve o'clock."

"This Saturday!" squealed Polly, nearly choking on her sparkle bar.

"That's a bit soon, isn't it?" said Daisy, concerned. "That's only a day away."

"Yes," said Holly, "shouldn't we have a trial run first?"

"There's no need," said Felicity, confidently. "The Big Wish will begin to work its magic right now!"

"But how in fairy world are you going to get the whole school together now?" said Polly, suspecting this was a very silly idea indeed.

"We don't have to get the whole school together!" said Felicity pleased with herself. "The Big Wish will be passed on from one fairy to another, until everyone in the whole school has done the same wish. There's nothing in the rules that says you all have to be in exactly the same place and make the wish at exactly the same time in order for it to work."

"That's brilliant!" said Holly.

Felicity was in her element. Blushing with pride she explained what each fairy would have to do to make the wish. Once every fairy had completed it, then at twelve o'clock on Saturday there would be rain.

"Rain?" asked Holly. "Why rain? Couldn't we all wish for a mountain of sweeties or make-overs for everyone in the school?"

"We have to show the judges that we're better than the Bird Island fairies to get into the world records. The easiest way to do this will be to do exactly the same thing only better. They had two hundred fairies, we shall have three hundred! They had rain, we shall have a tremendous downpour!"

* * *

Felicity, Holly, Polly and Daisy quickly set about spreading the word on how to make the Big Wish come true.

"Hold your wand above your head, spin round on the spot three times, wiggle your nose and wish with all your heart for heavy rain at twelve o'clock on Saturday!" whispered Felicity, Holly, Polly and Daisy to the fairies sitting next to them in Maths. "Pass it on!"

* * *

When they met that lunch-time under the Large Oak Tree each of the fairy friends had seen dozens of fairies whispering the Big Wish secret to someone else, and by the time they went into their next class, they'd seen even more fairies actually making the wish.

"This is really going to work!" whispered Polly to Felicity excitedly.

"I know!" said Felicity. "You can almost feel the magic in the air!"

"Psssstt…" hissed the fairy sitting next to Felicity. "Make this wish and then pass it on. Spin your wand around your head, wiggle your nose three times and wish with all your heart for something lovely."

Felicity went pale. It all sounded wrong.

"Are you sure you've got the instructions right?" whispered Felicity, to the fairy sitting next to her.

"Yes, that's what I was told. Oh, I almost forgot, make sure the wish comes true by midnight on Saturday." And the fairy winked.

Suddenly Felicity felt sick.

"Miss Sparkle," she burst out. "Please may I be excused from class? I'm not feeling too well."

* * *

When Holly and Polly found Felicity after class they discovered it wasn't excited butterflies that had turned her tummy, but worry.

"It might not matter that a lot of fairies have done the wish wrong," said Polly. "As long as most fairies get it right, everything should be fine," she continued encouragingly.

"Yes," said Holly. "We only really need two hundred and one fairies to break the world record."

"Why the sad faces?" said Daisy

happily as she sat down to join them. "Haven't you seen the clouds gathering outside? The Big Wish is about to come true!"

Felicity and her friends dashed outside and looked at the dark grey sky that was starting to envelop Little Blossoming. Quickly they flew home to get ready for tomorrow's Big Wish. At precisely twelve o'clock midnight the most enormous clap of thunder heralded the biggest downpour of rain Felicity had ever heard.

* * *

"It's a disaster!" said Felicity to her friends as they all sat wet and huddled round the table in Sparkles the next day. "The Fairy World Record judges will be here soon and it's still pouring with rain. What am I going to say?"

"You could pretend that they heard it wrong when you spoke to them on the phone, and that it was twelve o'clock last night and not twelve o'clock today that the wish was going to work," said Holly.

"Yes," said Daisy. "It's obviously an easy mistake to make!" she said, thinking of all the fairies that had made the same mix-up.

As they were talking, two very prim, well-dressed, stern-looking fairies entered the café.

"Hello!" called Felicity, waggling her wand. "Are you the Fairy World Record Judges?"

"Yes," replied one of them sharply. "Although I wish I wasn't on a day like this. I would have much rather stayed at home."

"I am Miss Point," said the other fairy, "and this is Miss Variable." She gestured to her colleague who was shaking her wet umbrella all over the floor.

"If you'd just like to fill in this form,
we have a few moments before your
Big Wish should come true."

Felicity looked awkward.

"You did say that in excess of two
hundred fairies took part in the wish,

didn't you?" she said flicking quickly through her notebook.

"Um, yes," said Felicity quickly.

"If the wish works we will need signed statements from all of them," said Miss Variable.

"And," said Miss Point, scanning down her list, "you did say that it would happen at twelve o'clock midday today."

Felicity winced. She was never any good at lying and just couldn't bring herself to pretend there had been a  mix-up. Miss Point looked at her watch.

"Four minutes to go. What exactly did you wish for anyway?" asked Miss Variable looking out of the window at the rainy weather.

Felicity didn't know where to begin, and didn't dare to explain to Miss

Point and Miss Variable
that she'd bought them
all the way to Sparkles
on a wasted journey.

As the hands on Miss Point's watch
slowly closed in on the number twelve,
something even more disastrous
happened. Up until then Felicity had
been hoping that at twelve o'clock
the rain might suddenly fall heavier
than it had before, or even better turn
into a storm.

But instead, as they all gazed out
of the window the rain silently began
to stop, until it was falling in a gentle
fine mist as delicate as Felicity's
teardrops.

"Goodness gracious," burst out Miss
Variable. "This is truly amazing! I've
never seen one like it."

Without stopping to explain, or get
her umbrella, she dashed out of the
doors and on to the street.

"It's wonderful!" sang Miss Point, a beaming smile transforming her face. "It's bigger than any one I've ever seen. I won't need to measure this! What you talented fairies have created with your Big Wish will doubtless be in The Book of Fairy World Records for decades to come!"

Standing in the doorway, Felicity wiped her eyes and looked up. There in the sky was the most vibrant, beautiful, big magical rainbow she had ever seen!

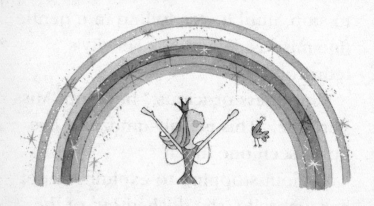

If you enjoyed this book, why not try another of these fantastic story collections?

Clutter Clean-out

Designer Drama

Newspaper Nerves

Star Surprise

Enchanted Escape

Friends Forever

Sensational Secrets

Whispering Wishes

Also available in the Felicity Wishes range:

Felicity Wishes: Mix-ups and Magic

Felicity makes a wish for each of her unhappy friends,
but her wishes are a little mixed-up...

Felicity Wishes: Snowflakes and Sparkledust

It is time for spring to arrive in Little Blossoming but there is a problem and
winter is staying put. Can Felicity Wishes get the seasons back on track?

Felicity Wishes: Secrets and Surprises

Felicity Wishes is planning her birthday party but it seems none of her friends can come. Will Felicity end up celebrating her birthday alone?

Felicity Wishes: Friendship and Fairyschool

It is nearly time for Felicity Wishes to leave fairy school. But poor Felicity has no idea what kind of fairy she wants to be!

Felicity Wishes has lots to say in
these fantastic little books:

Little Book of Love

Little Book of Peace

Little Book of Hiccups

Little Book of
Every Day Wishes

Little Book of Fun